WHAT MAKES A MAGNET?

BY FRANKLYN M. BRANLEY · ILLUSTRATED BY TRUE KELLEY

updated text by CAROLYN CINAMI DeCRISTOFANO

HARPER
An Imprint of HarperCollinsPublishers

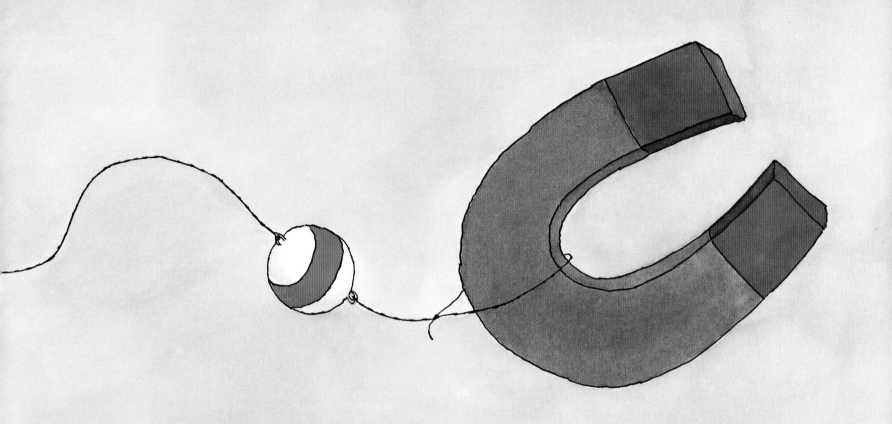

Let's go fishing with a magnet.

Put different things in a box: a twig and some tacks; a needle; paper clips and rubber bands; bits of paper and aluminum foil; a pin or two.

What else? You decide. Choose things that are small and light.

4

Next, find a magnet. They come in different shapes and sizes.

Tie one end of a string around your magnet. Tie the other end to a stick or a pencil. This is your fishing pole.

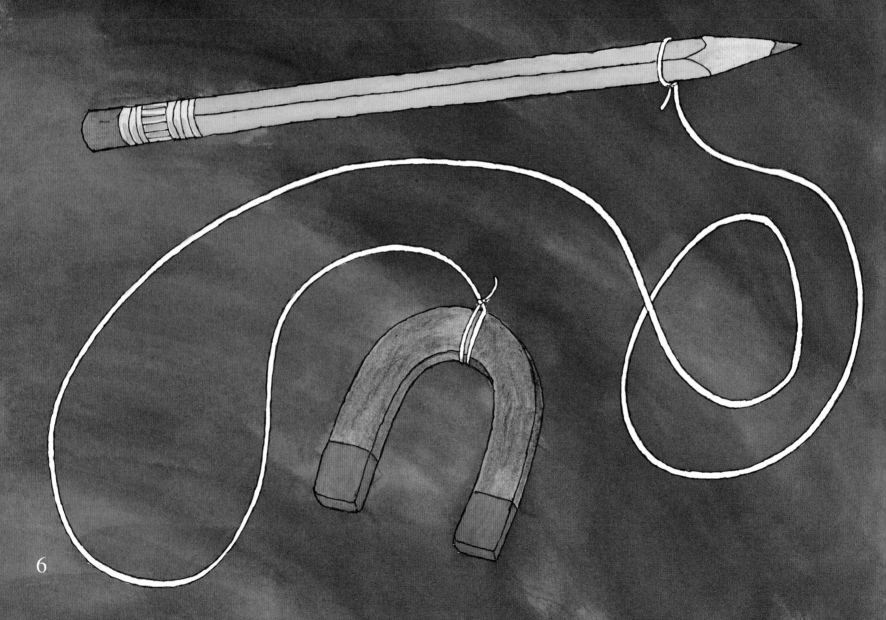

Go fishing in the box. Put the things you "catch"
in a pile. The others will stay in the box.

Maybe you caught the tacks, paper clips, needle, and pins but not the rubber bands and aluminum foil. There is a reason why only some things stick to the magnet. They have to be made of the right stuff.

The **material** they are made of has to be "magnet sticky," or **ferromagnetic**.

Anything you lifted out of the box probably has iron in it. The iron in these different objects is ferromagnetic. Iron is not the only ferromagnetic material, but it is the most common.

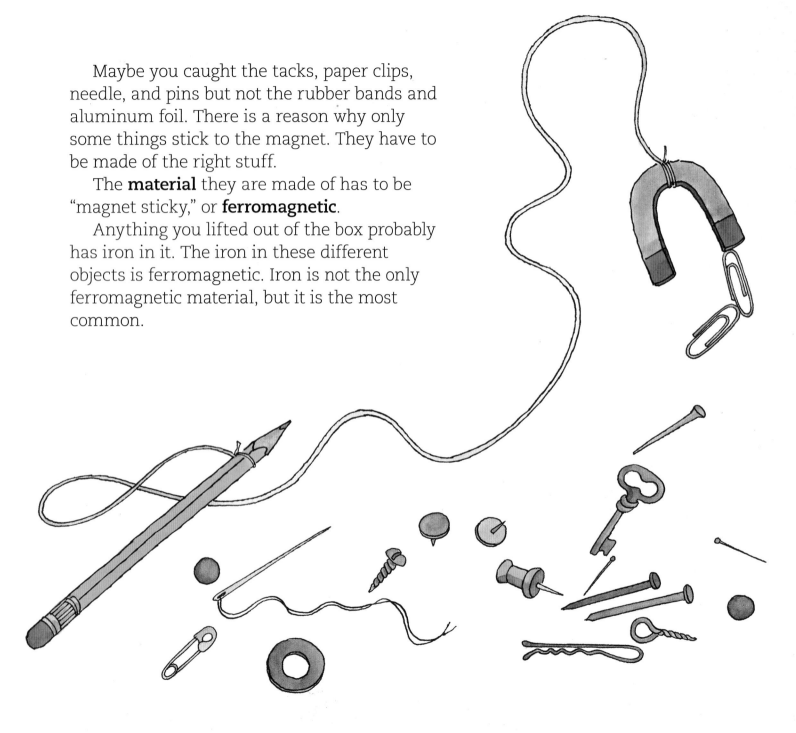

Can you tell which objects in your fishing expedition probably do *not* have ferromagnetic material in them? Need a hint? Look at what's still in your box!

The wood in a twig won't stick to a magnet. Wood is not ferromagnetic.

The rubber in the rubber bands won't stick to a magnet. Rubber is not ferromagnetic.

What about paper? Aluminum? Nope. They are not ferromagnetic, either.

There's something else about ferromagnetic materials. They can help you make a magnet. Want to try?

Start with a sewing needle. Make sure it can stick to the magnet. Place it on a table.

Hold it there with your finger on the needle's eye.

Handle the needle CAREFULLY so you don't stick your finger!

Needle's eye

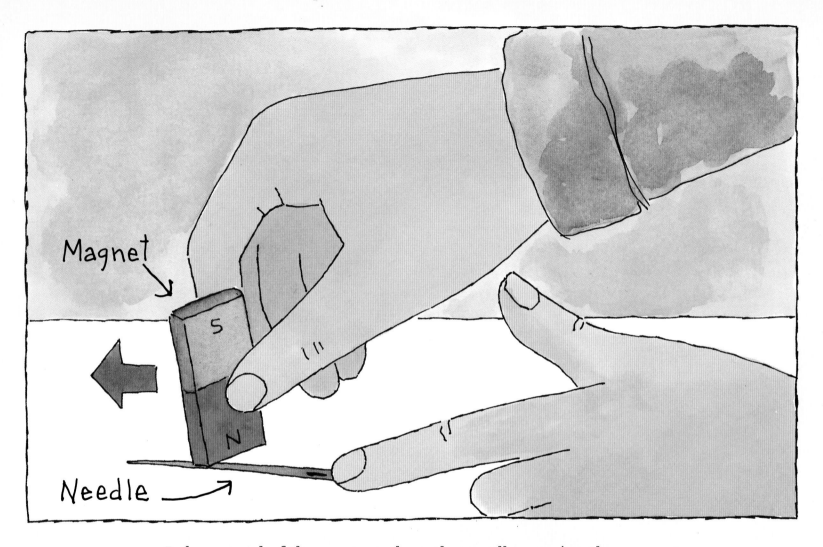

Rub one end of the magnet along the needle, moving the magnet from the eye of the needle to the point, not back and forth. Do this about thirty times.

Touch the needle tip to a tack, paper clip, or pin. If the object sticks to the needle, you have a new magnet. The **magnetized** needle might even be strong enough to pick up a few objects.

If your needle doesn't work as a magnet, try rubbing it a few more times. Remember to rub in only one direction.

The stronger a magnet is, the more it can pick up at once. Which do you think is stronger—your fishing magnet or the needle magnet? Try testing them to find out.

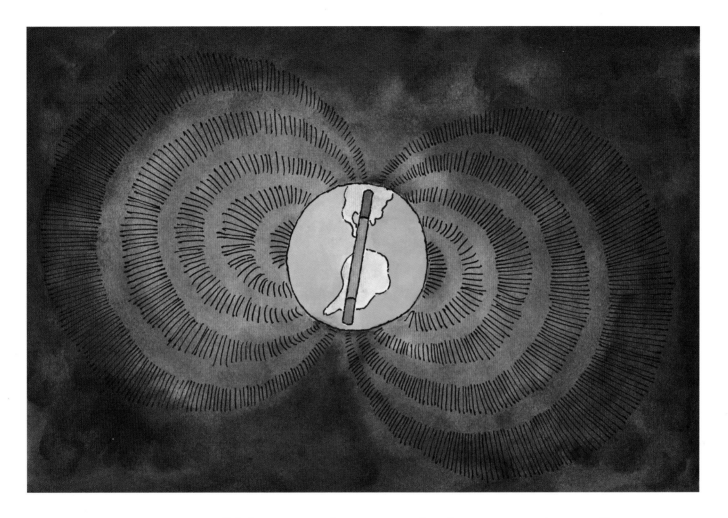

No matter which magnet is stronger, both magnets are small. They fit in your hand. But there are very large magnets, too.

In fact, the *whole world* is a magnet—even though it doesn't look like one.

You can't see the Earth's magnetism, but you can make something that shows you it is there: a **compass**.

1

Here's what to do.

Make sure your needle magnet still works. Then get two small pieces of foam, plastic, or cork. Carefully stick a piece on each end of your needle magnet.

CAREFUL— don't stick yourself.

CORK

NEEDLE MAGNET

CORK

2

Float the magnetized needle in a bowl of water. The needle will swing around so one end points north—the other end, south. Keep the needle in the center of the bowl so it can swing freely.

Turn the needle around. When you let go, the ends will point the same way as before. This happens because the needle magnet reacts to the Earth's magnetism.

3

To finish your compass, put a dot of ink on the north end of the needle.

4

Find North!

Think about where the sun sets. Stand facing that way. Keep this book in front of you.

My paw with the red glove points north. My other paw points south.

SOUTH

NORTH

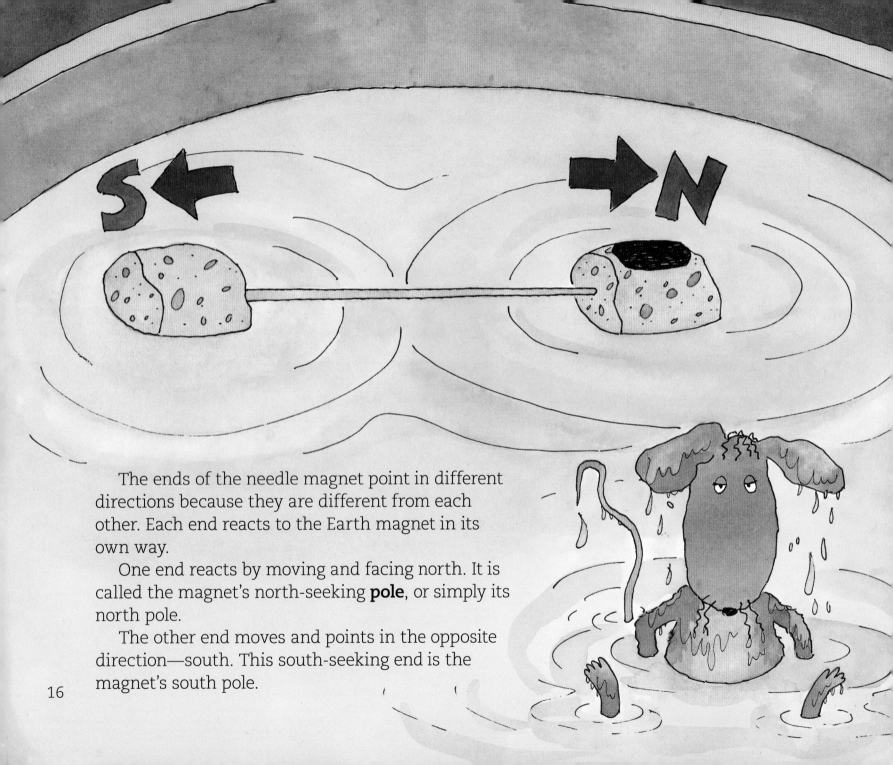

The ends of the needle magnet point in different directions because they are different from each other. Each end reacts to the Earth magnet in its own way.

One end reacts by moving and facing north. It is called the magnet's north-seeking **pole**, or simply its north pole.

The other end moves and points in the opposite direction—south. This south-seeking end is the magnet's south pole.

16

Magnets are strongest at their poles. When you picked things out of your fishing box, they stuck to the ends of the magnet, not the middle.

Poles make magnets work. Magnets make compasses work. And compasses help people find their way around the block or around the world.

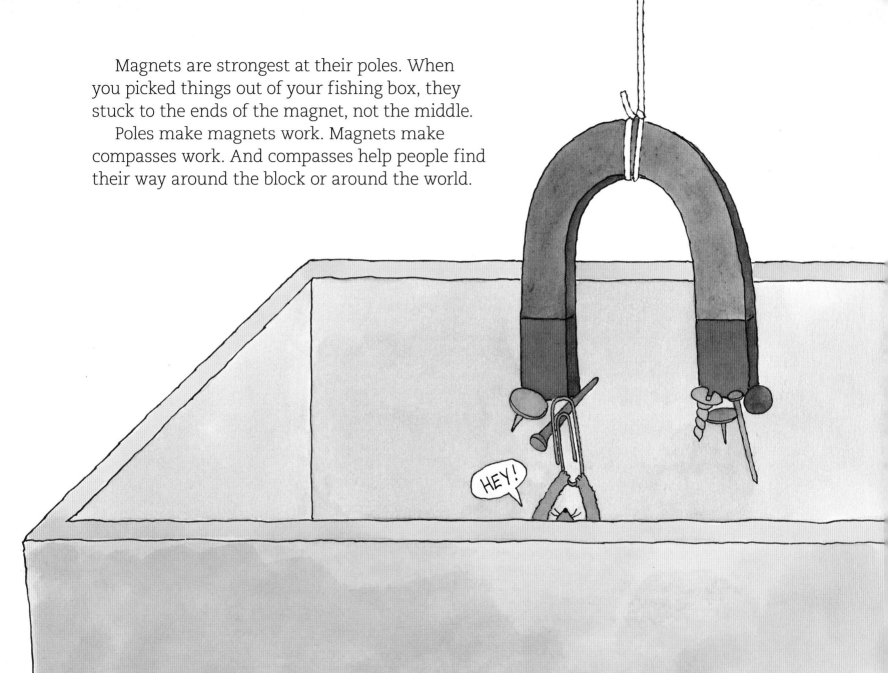

Before compasses, people got lost a lot. How were compasses invented?

No one knows the whole story. For sure, it began a long, long time ago.

In **ancient** times, people from different parts of the world knew of an unusual stone.

Iron stuck to it. It could be used to make new magnets from iron.

And, when the stone was used as a spinner, it came to rest with one end facing north and the other south. This natural magnet stone was important for making compasses.

Some people called this magnet stone **lodestone**, which means "leading stone" or "guide stone." You can see why.

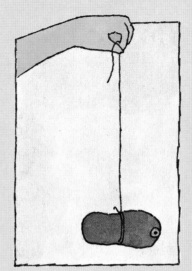

Lodestone Compass

Some compasses were very simple—magnetized needles or lodestones hanging from a thread. They turned and pointed like your compass needle.

Fish Compass

One compass from long ago used magnetized iron shaped like a fish. When it was placed in a bowl of water, the fish floated and lined up north–south.

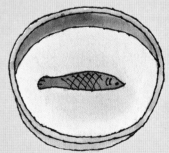

Nowadays, sailors, hikers, and pilots use different types of compasses to track where they are going.

Compasses helped explorers travel the world. They returned home with new ideas, food, and art. So much happened because people were curious about magnets!

Now it's *your* turn to explore some more.

Can you use your magnet to push the needle magnet in the water—without letting the two magnets touch? Try it!

When the needle magnet moves away from the magnet in your hand, both magnets' north or south poles face each other. Their similar poles push apart. Either way works—north facing north or south facing south. Similar poles always **repel**.

Try making the needle magnet "swim" toward the other magnet. North and south poles pull toward each other. Unlike poles always **attract**.

Does magnetism work through paper or cardboard? Test and find out.

How far from a pin can you hold a magnet and still attract the pin? Try it and see.

What else do you want to try?

You *could* try making a magnet from a penny or a wooden toothpick—but that won't work. Remember? Some metals are not ferromagnetic and neither is wood. Only ferromagnetic materials can be magnetized. This is because of something too tiny to see.

Picture the smallest bits of iron in your needle. They are like tiny magnets. Usually, they point in different directions. When you stroke a magnet along a needle, the iron bits line up—the magnetism of one **particle** is added to another, making the magnetism stronger.

BEFORE

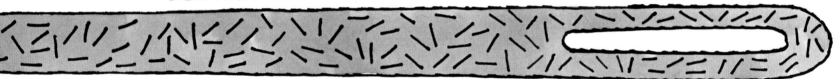

AFTER

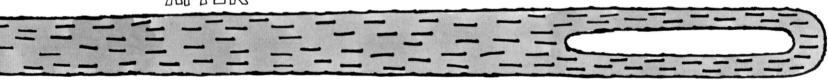

That explains what happens when you make a magnet. But lodestone is a *natural* magnet. Nobody made it. What can make a natural magnet?

Lightning!
A bolt of lightning has magnetism. Lodestone has a lot of iron in it. A lightning strike on the right iron-filled rock can act like lots and lots of magnet strokes all at once. **Scientists** are pretty sure that lightning struck the places where lodestone is found and changed ordinary stone into magnetic stone.

Now you know a lot of what scientists know about magnetism. Even so, sometimes it still seems magical. After all, it goes through air and water, glass and plastic, walls and tabletops.

Enjoy this feeling of wonder.

Keep exploring with your magnets like a scientist and see what else you can find out.

Go on a Magnetic **Technology** Scavenger Hunt!

Magnetism makes all sorts of useful things work. How many of these magnet-using technologies do you use? How many can you find?

Directions: Look for these magnet-using technologies in real life or pictures. As you find them, check them off the list.

- ❏ Freezer (Magnets under the plastic seal keep your freezer door closed tight.)
- ❏ Refrigerator magnets keep notes and pictures handy.
- ❏ Hair dryer
- ❏ Electric drill
- ❏ Vacuum cleaner
- ❏ Cell phone
- ❏ Any toy with a motor (train, helicopter, walking doll)
- ❏ Headphones
- ❏ Computer
- ❏ Microphone
- ❏ School bus
- ❏ ATM machine
- ❏ X-ray machine to look at people's bones and other body parts so they stay healthy

If you like thinking about these technologies, you might grow up to be an **engineer**. Lots of engineers invent helpful things that use magnetism.

This book meets the Common Core State Standards for Science and Technical Subjects. For Common Core resources for this title and others, please visit www.readcommoncore.com.

Glossary

Ancient—from very long ago; very old

Attract—make something move closer

Compass—an object that has a magnetic needle in it and helps people find north and south, especially when they travel

Engineer—a problem-solving person who uses math, science, and ideas to improve or invent technologies

Ferromagnetic—magnet sticky, or strongly attracted to magnets. Iron and most steel are examples of ferromagnetic materials.

Lodestone—a type of rock that naturally attracts iron and other ferromagnetic materials; a natural magnet

Magnetized—made into a magnet

Material—what something is made of. Some examples of materials are: plastic, cardboard, cloth, glass, wood, and metal.

Particle—a tiny bit of something

Poles—the parts of a magnet where its magnetism is strongest

Repel—make something move away

Scientist—a person who learns by wondering, making predictions, exploring, and carefully noticing and tracking what happens

Technology—anything created by people to be useful or solve a problem

Be sure to look for all of these books in the **Let's-Read-and-Find-Out Science** series:

The Human Body: (Level 1)
How Many Teeth?
I'm Growing!
My Feet
My Five Senses
My Hands
Sleep Is for Everyone
What's For Lunch?

Plants and Animals:
Animals in Winter
Baby Whales Drink Milk
Big Tracks, Little Tracks
Bugs Are Insects
Dinosaurs Big and Small
Ducks Don't Get Wet
Fireflies in the Night
From Caterpillar to Butterfly
From Seed to Pumpkin
From Tadpole to Frog
How Animal Babies Stay Safe
How a Seed Grows
A Nest Full of Eggs
Starfish
A Tree Is a Plant
What Lives in a Shell?
What's Alive?
What's It Like to Be a Fish?
Where Are the Night Animals?
Where Do Chicks Come From?

The World Around Us:
Air Is All Around You
The Big Dipper
Clouds
Is There Life in Outer Space?
Pop!
Snow Is Falling
Sounds All Around
What Makes a Shadow?

The Human Body: (Level 2)
A Drop of Blood
Germs Make Me Sick!
Hear Your Heart
The Skeleton Inside You
What Happens to a Hamburger?
Why I Sneeze, Shiver, Hiccup, and Yawn
Your Skin and Mine

Plants and Animals:
Almost Gone
Ant Cities
Be a Friend to Trees
Chirping Crickets
Corn Is Maize
Dolphin Talk
Honey in a Hive
How Do Apples Grow?
How Do Birds Find Their Way?
Life in a Coral Reef
Look Out for Turtles!
Milk from Cow to Carton
An Octopus Is Amazing
Penguin Chick
Sharks Have Six Senses
Snakes Are Hunters
Spinning Spiders
Sponges Are Skeletons
What Color Is Camouflage?
Who Eats What?
Who Lives in an Alligator Hole?
Why Do Leaves Change Color?
Why Frogs Are Wet
Wiggling Worms at Work
Zipping, Zapping, Zooming Bats

Dinosaurs:
Did Dinosaurs Have Feathers?
Digging Up Dinosaurs
Dinosaur Bones
Dinosaur Tracks
Dinosaurs Are Different
Fossils Tell of Long Ago
My Visit to the Dinosaurs
What Happened to the Dinosaurs?
Where Did Dinosaurs Come From?

Space:
Floating in Space
The International Space Station
Mission to Mars
The Moon Seems to Change
The Planets in Our Solar System
The Sky Is Full of Stars
The Sun
What Makes Day and Night
What the Moon Is Like

Weather and the Seasons:
Down Comes the Rain
Feel the Wind
Flash, Crash, Rumble, and Roll
Hurricane Watch
Sunshine Makes the Seasons
Tornado Alert
What Will the Weather Be?

Our Earth:
Archaeologists Dig for Clues
Earthquakes
Follow the Water from Brook to Ocean
How Mountains Are Made
In the Rainforest
Let's Go Rock Collecting
Oil Spill!
Volcanoes
What Happens to Our Trash?
What's So Bad About Gasoline?
Where Do Polar Bears Live?
Why Are the Ice Caps Melting?
You're Aboard Spaceship Earth

The World Around Us:
Day Light, Night Light
Energy Makes Things Happen
Forces Make Things Move
Gravity Is a Mystery
How People Learned to Fly
Light Is All Around Us
Simple Machines
Switch On, Switch Off
What Is the World Made Of?
What Makes a Magnet?
Where Does the Garbage Go?

Special thanks to Dr. Zoran Ninkov, Professor of Astrophysical Sciences and Technology, Chester F. Carlson Center for Imaging Science, Rochester Institute of Technology, for his valuable assistance.

The Let's-Read-and-Find-Out Science book series was originated by Dr. Franklyn M. Branley, Astronomer Emeritus and former Chairman of the American Museum of Natural History–Hayden Planetarium, and was formerly co-edited by him and Dr. Roma Gans, Professor Emeritus of Childhood Education, Teachers College, Columbia University. Text and illustrations for each of the books in the series are checked for accuracy by an expert in the relevant field. For more information about Let's-Read-and-Find-Out Science books, write to HarperCollins Children's Books, 195 Broadway, New York, NY 10007, or visit our website at www.letsreadandfindout.com.

The artist used watercolor and pen and ink on Fabriano watercolor paper to create the illustrations for this book.
Typography by Erica De Chavez
15 16 17 18 19   SCP   10 9 8 7 6 5 4 3 2 1
❖
Revised Edition, 2016

When participating in activities in this book, it is important to keep safety in mind. Several experiments in the book call for the use of small or sharp objects, which could present a choking hazard. Magnets can also affect credit and debit cards, computers, and any device with a screen, so children should be instructed to keep magnets away from these objects.

Children should always ask permission from an adult before doing any of the activities and should be supervised by an adult at all times. The publisher, author, and artist disclaim any liability from any injury that might result from the participation, proper or improper, of the activities contained in this book.